# Rise of the Mooncusser

KEN MCALPINE

ISBN: **0991033434**
ISBN-13: **978-0991033430**

# DEDICATION

To those who see progress for both her warts and her charms.

ACKNOWLEDGMENTS

Special thanks to Hank Tovar cover design

# 1 THE WHALER

The man had come to her as if in a trance. He had taken no pleasure in the act. When he finished, he wept. He was an ugly man and his hands smelled of ruined meat, as a whaler's hands do, but Salem had stopped caring about the appearance or touch of her customers. When he finished telling his story, she held him while they both cried. Later she heard he had left the Cape, disappearing completely.

Before they parted she told him that life goes on, it always had. She was young, and knew no better.

He stared at her, a naked scarecrow with eyes gone out.

"It's a sickness inside me, a black ugliness like a storm that doesn't pass," he said. "I can never again have faith in this world."

It was surprisingly poetic for an ugly man who had spent his life on whaling ships.

It was a horrible story, yet as time passed Salem Wyman's curiosity grew to be unbearable.

This, she thought, is a man who will stop at nothing. I must know him.

# 2 WINDS OF CHANGE

The summer of 1870 brought fog and shipwrecks and winds of change. The good citizens of Cape Cod welcomed two of the three.

Daniel Cole received notification of a profound change in his own life in the form of a brief letter, delivered wordlessly by Obed Shiverick and his sway-backed mule on a still July afternoon.

"That man may be the only person on the Cape who says less than you," Sara observed.

They stood outside the cabin, watching the sullen mail carrier ride off down the narrow path through the woods.

"I've tried just about everything to get him to speak more than three words and three words is the best I've done. 'Morning, Mrs.Cole.' I hold out hope, one day, for a 'Good morning'."

Daniel Cole gave a small smile.

"Silence is an undervalued trait," he said.

"*You* think so because it gives you an excuse to stand around and say nothing. I wonder what that man says to his wife."

"It's possible she does most of the talking."

Sara was slender, but she delivered an appreciable cuff.

"Women talk because they wish to be *part* of this world. They want to *learn* things. They want to *communicate* and *share*. They want to know the men who presumably love them."

They stood alone in the dappled tree shadows, but Sara did not miss how her husband glanced about.

"I do love you," he said.

"It would be too much for me to hope you might shout that to the heavens."

Cole peered up through the leafy canopy to the pale sky.

"I love this woman," he said softly.

"My. Have you always been this demonstrative?"

"Yes. See? We are getting to know each other."

When she cocked her head, her hair caught the sunlight. Daniel loved her hair. Black as midnight, it felt like cool water between his fingers.

"Have you always been this maddening?"

"I don't know. It's possible you'll tell me."

She cuffed him again.

"My arm's going numb," he said. "I won't be able to open the letter."

"Please. From what I've seen, there's only one occasion where you feel anything."

Suddenly that was all he wanted. He had spent the morning at the Wellfleet dock making repairs to the skipjack. He couldn't go fishing. The seams required time to cure. It forced the rarest day off, and he knew how he wanted to spend it.

He looked again at his wife. They had been married for three years and he could never get enough of her. He knew that was the way it would always be.

The thought made him smile.

"What?"

"I really do love you."

"Thank you, William Shakespeare."

He kissed her slowly.

When they separated she said, "Shakespeare had his strengths and you have yours."

Already trembling, she took his hand.

"I should open the letter," he said.

"It can wait," she said, but she knew it wouldn't.

He carefully opened the letter at the kitchen table. Sara stood behind him, her hands resting on his shoulders. A cursory glance revealed Daniel Cole to be a touch shorter than the average man. A quiet manner led many to further overlook him. But she alone touched his body and so knew the power residing there.

He read the letter as she knew he would, silently and with absolute focus.

When he finished, he raised his head. For a moment he said nothing, staring past the tidy sitting room, out through the window and the break in the trees to Shetland Pond, glittering in the afternoon sun.

"It's from the United States Lifesaving Service in Washington. They want me to be Keeper of the Peaked Hill Bars station."

It did not surprise her. He was the perfect choice.

"You're the perfect choice," she said.

Folding the letter neatly, he slipped it into the envelope. Standing, he took her in his arms.

"I know you don't want me to take the job."

"I want what you want."

She said it because she meant it, but she also knew he had already decided.

"I want you to be happy," he said.

"Well then, you have to promise you won't do anything rash."

When her husband did smile it was like a summer sunrise.

"I fear I'm going to break that promise immediately."

The news changed their lovemaking, as it would change their lives.

When Sara woke in the blue-black of evening's last night, she saw the light under the door. She knew her husband was at the kitchen table crafting his letter of acceptance.

The next morning Cole rode into Wellfleet, delivering the letter to the post office himself.

News of the selection of Keepers swept across the Cape: it was the next step in the succession of steps designed to make the dangerous shores of Cape Cod a safer place.

The United States Lifesaving Service had decided to build nine stations along the Cape, from Monomoy in the south to Race Point near

Provincetown. It was a decision that could no longer be postponed. So many had died already. In winter shipwrecks occurred on average once every two to three weeks, but a bad storm could cast several ships upon the treacherous offshore shoals in a matter of hours. An 1864 report to the Massachusetts State Legislature had counted 827 wrecks along the Cape over the previous seventeen years. Cole and everyone else on the Cape knew this to be a highly conservative estimate. It was true, the Massachusetts Humane Society had long had shelters along the coast, rickety structures, little bigger than an outhouse, stocked with firewood and a small amount of supplies, but amidst the hell of winter's shrieking gales it was the lucky shipwreck victim who made it ashore, much less found their way to a shelter.

The village cemeteries brimmed with unmarked graves.

Finally the United States Lifesaving Service had decided this had gone on long enough. They had started building the stations at the first sign of spring. They were to be completed, and fully manned, in time for winter's storms.

Daniel Cole waited until Sunday before setting out for Provincetown. After penning his letter of acceptance, he had stayed up the rest of the night. Beneath lantern light, he made notes and decisions. When dawn's gray crept among the trees he had his list.

He and Sara left together in the buckboard as they always did. Sara worshipped each Sunday at the Presbyterian Church in Provincetown. Cole always brought her into town in the wagon, walking her halfway across the church yard before saying goodbye. He had never put any faith in religion; marrying a devout woman hadn't changed things. For a time Sara had tried to win him over, but then she had let it go. It was one of the few matters in which he refused to acquiesce to her.

After dropping his wife at church, most Sundays Cole continued down Bradford Street to Provincetown Harbor where he walked the docks or simply sat and looked out at the water. He liked how the worldly commerce made him feel small and inconsequential, the vast rows of cod and mackerel shimmering in silver columns, salted and drying in the sun, the whaling ships from New Bedford gathering their last supplies before sailing for the Pacific whaling grounds, the men hurrying past as if he didn't exist. Occasionally he guided the horse and wagon up the steep hill to Provincetown Cemetery, where he sat in the shade of a lone white oak, gazing out over Provincetown's jumbled buildings to the blue-green expanse of Cape Cod Bay.

He always returned to the Presbyterian Church twenty minutes after the service ended. In summer, Sara waited on the bench bordering Gosnold Street. In winter, she watched for him through the stained glass window at the church entrance. Punctual in all matters, Cole returned late to avoid the Reverend Marmaduke Matthews. For some inexplicable reason the fiery orator with the booming voice had taken on Cole's conversion as a personal crusade. To Cole it was annoying enough that the minister found it necessary to meddle in his personal life; it was made more annoying still by Cole's distaste for the man. Regarding this matter, Sara had not conceded defeat. She found Reverend Matthews' sermons, while a bit histrionic, inspiring. Repeatedly, she tried to discern why her husband detested the minister so. Cole couldn't give a reason, mostly because he couldn't pinpoint one himself, and so it went on and on, one of the few flies in the ointment of their marital bliss.

Today Cole turned the horse toward the docks. It was a quiet morning, touched with cool. He looked forward to sorting through his selections a final time, while the waters beneath the docks ran around the pilings making their soft sighings.

Two boys ducked into an alley ahead. The trailing boy saw him and looked away. Cole knew both boys, troublemakers whose fathers drank more often than they fished.

He wanted nothing more than a quiet hour on the docks. He flicked the reins once, and then reluctantly gave them a pull.

He hitched the horse in front of the blacksmith's shop, the windows blackened at the edges. He glimpsed his reflection. In the dusty glass he looked like a boy himself.

Cole turned into the alley.

Someone swore.

Five boys stared at him from the back of the alley. The boys stood around a barrel. A slender man crouched atop the barrel, his knees drawn tightly to his chest. The man wore only long johns, sorely patched. Blackened skin showed through holes yet to be patched. In all seasons, Ezekiel Donne wandered the dunes in his underthings.

In the confines of the alley, Cole smelled the faint tang of urine.

Cole stood silent, feeling a little sad.

The largest boy attempted bravado.

"Leave us alone."

Cole knew this boy too. He was older than the others, nearly twenty. Cole tried to remember his name.

"Ezekiel. You may go."

The slim man with the gold hair shifted atop the barrel. Freeing a leg, he waved a bare foot off the barrel's edge as if testing the water, but he did not descend. Even in this awkward position he was strangely beautiful and delicate, like some woodland nymph.

Pale blue eyes continued to watch the boys with fear.

A dark-haired boy Cole did not recognize said, "He's so scared he pissed himself."

"Fear in others breeds courage in cowards," Cole said.

Nearby a dog howled.

Ezekiel slowly swung his leg back and forth like a divining rod.

"Evil boys," he said.

The dark-haired boy spat on the side of the barrel.

"Circus freak."

"Enough," said Cole.

Fear had entered the eyes of all the boys but one.

"He's a half-wit," said the dark-haired boy. "An animal. No different from the dog. He stank before we found him."

"He is no different from us. The rest of you go. Don't let me catch you at anything like this again."

Eyes downcast, the four boys slid past. At the alley entrance, they ran.

Crouched on the barrel, Ezekiel looked at Cole hopefully.

"Beat him. Beat him with your fists."

"That would be no different than what they did to you, Ezekiel."

"Beat him until he begs. Cries like a little boy." He smiled at the boy. "Now *you* are afraid."

The boy stepped close to the barrel.

"I'll find you again, freak."

Ezekiel chuckled.

"No. You won't."

"You're goddamn crazy."

The boy stepped back before turning to Cole.

"Who are you?"

"It doesn't matter."

"We were just having fun."

"I'm going to tell you something you'll remember again one day."

"What?"

"You're as happy now as you're ever going to be."

Cole stepped aside.

"Go."

The boy slouched past. At the entrance to the alley, he turned and shouted a curse.

Cole did not turn around. He had rarely been so close to Ezekiel Donne. Though his skin, in parts, was ruined, his thick hair fairly glowed. With his fine-boned face and soft blue eyes, he was pretty like a woman. Cole was surprised by how young he was; little older than the boys who had cornered him.

Ezekiel slipped soundlessly from the barrel.

"You watch the ships," he said.

"I do."

"I watch them too. They come to bad ends."

Ezekiel Donne left, trailing the scent of urine.

On this Sunday, Cole returned to church as the service was letting out.

He waited at the far edge of the lawn. Cloaked in white vestments, Marmaduke Matthews stood on the front stoop of the church greeting the departing parishioners. Even at a distance the man's size was obvious. To Cole he looked like his own snowfall.

Sara was one of the first parishioners to shake the Reverend's hand and descend down the steps. Even here, beneath the very eye of God, he noticed her slim hips and animal grace.

The way she smiled spilled something warm inside him.

"Well now Daniel, I wish I could say you're here early because you've finally decided to accept our Lord, but I know today's prayers didn't change things either. How was your communing?"

"Brief. I'm hoping to speak to Martin Nelson. Did you see him at the service?"

"I did. The man is God-fearing, steadfastly loyal and hard to miss. Why do you want to see him?"

"For the last two reasons," said Cole.

"Well there's your man."

Cole watched Martin Nelson step forward and take Reverend Matthews' hand. Although Martin was the only parishioner larger than the minister, Cole saw how the Swede stooped, vainly attempting to make himself smaller as he quickly shook the minister's hand.

Head still down, the Swede made his way with equal rapidity down the stairs and across the lawn.

Cole cut him off just as he reached the street.

"Martin."

Reluctantly, the big man stopped and turned.

When he saw Cole he stood up straight and grinned.

"Mr. Cole. It's a pleasant surprise to see you."

By Cole's guess, Martin was in his mid-twenties. Less than eight years probably separated them, and they knew each other well from fishing the same waters, but from their first meeting Martin had always addressed him in the same formal fashion. Cole had tried to get the Swede to use his first name, but once Martin was stuck on something it was impossible to get him to change course. Sundays excepted, the Swede was at the dock at precisely four each morning and he never came in early.

It was why his name had been first on the list.

Martin still grinned.

"Daniel Cole not at the grindstone?"

"I decided to skip fishing and follow you home to sample one of those famous pies. I have a wife now," he added unnecessarily.

"I can see that." He could. Martin towered over the parishioners now streaming past, some of them casting sidelong glances at Cole. "Mrs. Cole is very beautiful."

"Yes she is. Thank you."

"I do bake on Sundays. I would be honored if you and your wife came by."

"Thank you, but not today."

"Some other day then," said Martin, though both men knew that day would never come.

Cole did not traffic in regret.

"I've a proposal for you, Martin," he said.

Martin Nelson did not hesitate in accepting Cole's offer, but Willie Bangs did, as Cole knew he would.

Cole also knew where he would find Willie Bangs on a Sunday morning. Again Cole turned the wagon down Bradford Street, Sara swaying beside him. He did not want to bring his wife into the Cork and Barrel, but he knew she wouldn't wait outside.

As he helped her down from the wagon she said, "So this is where you go when I'm praying for you. It seems I'll have to pray harder."

"This shouldn't take long," said Cole, although his already sinking heart told him nothing was quick with Willie Bangs.

"And who, pray tell, are you propositioning here, Keeper Cole?"

"Willie Bangs."

"Is that so?"

"Yes," said Cole, wondering again if he should change his mind. "That's so."

Sara laughed.

"Well it's quite the spectrum of crew you're assembling. First a pious Swede who answers to God, and now a man who answers to no one. What in God's name is that?"

She had stopped in her tracks.

Cole looked up at the weather-beaten buffalo head above the door. The buffalo ignored them, choosing instead to stare disconsolately in the general direction of Provincetown Harbor. Snow, rain and freeze had turned the beast riotously unkempt, appropriate given what waited inside.

"That would be Rummy's idea of a good luck charm," said Cole.

"The animal seems to have experienced no luck at all. Any reason it is cross-eyed?"

"The taxidermist is a regular customer," said Cole, holding open the door.

Thankfully, Sunday mornings were quiet. The bar was almost empty. A scattering of customers sat at the few tables. One table was occupied by four young whores. A man slept upright in a chair against the far wall, snoring loudly.

They stood for a moment, letting their eyes adjust. It was, as always, dim inside. Lanterns hung from the low ceiling beams, but only two of them were lit. Oil was costly. The Cork and Barrel was owned by Rummy McGuiness, a mole of a man famous for his stinginess.

Ladies were a rarity in the Cork and Barrel. As they stepped inside all eyes but the snorer's turned to Sara.

Sara gave the room a pleasant nod.

"A fine Sunday morning to all."

As they passed the table of whores, a plump, bright-eyed woman with a head full of pretty blond curls chimed, "Top of the morning to you too, ma'am."

Willie Bangs sat alone. He was playing solitaire, shot glass, nearly empty bottle of whisky and a rolled up newspaper arranged neatly on the table.

Whether he had looked up as they entered was hard to tell. Whether he was looking up now was hard to tell. The man sported a cascade of barely tamed hair. What hair didn't fall past his shoulders and elsewhere, lay over his eyes. To Sara it appeared that a sheep dog in ruined overalls was playing cards.

When they arrived at the table, a hand pushed aside the necessary amount of hair, revealing merry blue eyes.

"Daniel Cole," said Willie Bangs, rising. He tapped a finger to the Boston Herald. "They'll have to print a second edition. This is front page news."

"May we sit?"

Willie stepped around to pull out a chair.

"I insist. Always a pleasure to see you Mrs. Cole, although it's a particular pleasure to see you in your Sunday finery."

"Thank you, Mr. Bangs."

Cole wasn't sure if his wife blushed or whether she had applied a bit too much rouge.

Willie raised a hand in the direction of the bar, but Cole shook his head.

"We're not here to drink."

"Given it is a saloon, I hope you don't mind if I do."

Willie poured a last shot, giving the empty bottle a long look.

"I believe Rummy is purchasing smaller bottles. How did you find today's sermon, Mrs. Cole?"

"The race is not to the swift, nor the battle to the strong, neither yet bread to the wise, or yet riches to men of understanding, nor yet favor to men of skill; but time and chance happeneth to them all."

"Hedging one's bets, I would say."

Sara laughed.

"You'd have to take that up with Ecclesiastes, Mr. Bangs."

"Well I do fancy an egalitarian outlook. So what brings your husband here? I do see him occasionally, disappearing over the horizon to catch fish no one else can find or, on Sundays, wandering about the wharves looking for something I doubt he'll ever find. You'll be happy to know he never frequents this den of inequity."

"He is a good man, even without God."

"One hopes the church door isn't the only door," said Willie.

"I'm here to ask you if you want the job as my number one surfman," said Cole.

Willie Bangs put the whisky down.

"With every passing second the morning turns stranger," he said.

Cole did not want the conversation to wiggle away from him again.

"You are aware of the lifesaving stations?" he asked.

"I'm a wee bit tipsy, but I'm not blind."

"Then you know they'll be completed by the end of August."

"Not if the men I know remain on the construction crews."

Once again, the man was hijacking the conversation. Cole had known Willie since they were boys. They had been friends, but even then Willie had thrown him off-kilter.

As if reading his mind, Willie sat back.

"I heard the sage minds in Washington picked John Kilbride to head the Race Point station," he said. "Interesting, assigning the wolf to guard the chicken coop."

"I have been appointed Keeper at Peaked Hill Bars."

He was only trying to regain control of the conversation, but it sounded like a boast in his ears.

He waited for Willie to pounce on the opportunity.

Instead Willie said, "Well at least one person in Washington knows what they're doing."

"I am asking you to be second in command."

"I hope that's not your best selling point, Daniel. I'm even less keen on bossing than having a boss."

Willie Bangs was one of the best trap fishermen on the Cape. Few men knew the Cape's waters better. He had served bravely during the Civil War, fighting in some of the war's most vicious battles. But now Cole wondered if he was making a grand mistake.

Before he could say anything, Sara placed a hand gently on Willie's arm.

"My husband is trying very hard to offer you a job."

"I realize he is, Mrs. Cole. It's just that he's taken me aback. And when taken aback, my thoughts tend to scatter."

"I'm offering a steady wage," said Cole.

"And abysmally steady hours, not to mention a better than fair shot at debilitating injury and death."

Both men saw Sara stiffen.

"Apologies, Mrs. Cole," said Willie, "but we all know it's true." He turned to Cole. "You are aware that not all our citizenry welcomes the coming of your lifesaving stations. Honesty being the best policy, I am among them."

Life on the Cape was hard. Many supplemented what meager income they gained from fishing or farming by scavenging what good misfortune brought them. A wrecked ship meant wood and iron, ship's wheels, spars, deadeyes, shackles, chock cleats and nails. Sails, rigging, and nets were hauled back to barns, repaired, and resold. Iron was reforged. Across the Cape, wagons filled with knives, axes, and crowbars waited at the ready. News of a grounded ship traveled like buckshot and it was first come, first served.

If the lifesavers freed a grounded ship, that largesse would sail off to the horizon.

"I'm not engaged in a popularity contest," said Cole.

"You are certainly not."

Cole was tired of the banter. He fell silent.

Across the bar the snorer fell off his chair, producing a resounding clatter and shout. Re-seating himself with dignity, he fell promptly back to sleep.

"Must be a good dream," observed Willie. He gave the empty whisky bottle a forlorn poke. "Buy me another drink."

"No."

Cole stood, moving to Sara's chair before Willie could.

"My offer stands until Tuesday morning."

Outside Cole said, "I'm sorry you had to sit through that."

"I rather enjoyed it."

"I should have let you talk to him then." Settling himself beside his wife, Cole took up the reins. "That man is exasperating."

"He's also amusing and oddly attractive in an unkempt sort of way."

Now it was her husband's turn to stiffen.

"Oh Daniel." She kissed his cheek. "No one holds a candle to you. You know it's possible he was toying with you."

"I have always been an easy target."

An elderly woman, finely dressed, waved a gloved hand in their direction.

"I'm relieved that Mrs. Chisholm didn't see us leaving your Cork and Barrel," said Sara returning the wave. "*That* would raise a ruckus amongst the Provincetown bridge club."

Cole was barely listening.

"I doubt he'll take the job," he said. "Now that I think about it, it was foolish. I can't see him working for anybody, much less me."

"Don't be so certain. They say that opposites attract."

Willie sent word to Cole on Monday afternoon, the note delivered by a young nephew.

Again Sara stood behind her husband as he opened the envelope at the kitchen table.

Three words were scrawled across the wrinkled piece of paper.

*Reluctantly, I accept.*

Cole looked up at his wife.

"Proof, yet again," he said, "that women are wiser than men."

# 3 KNIGHT

Pomp could see the whaler was drunker than most, which on a Saturday night in the Cork and Barrel was a distinction of note. Pomp first noticed the man in a brief skirmish near the bar. It ended quickly, as alcohol-induced skirmishes do. The loser, knocked cold and bleeding profusely from the left temple where the bottle had shattered, was carried out. The blow had been swift. Pomp saw that the man bestowing the blow didn't care whether his opponent was rendered senseless or dispatched from this life.

Pomp didn't care either. Seated at his usual table, on this night he was having the finest luck with cards. For three hours now he had emptied the pockets of a succession of challengers and his luck was still holding, which was why Pomp gave the whaler only sidelong consideration. Normally, Pomp paid the whalers no attention at all. But drunkenness alone did not distinguish this man. He was different. A predator knows a predator.

Yet when he saw the man go upstairs with the plump young whore Abby Hierdal, Pomp gave it no thought, and later, when the man came down the stairs slightly faster than he'd ascended, Pomp ignored him again. It was the whaler's bad luck that he did not depart immediately.

When Rummy McGuinness left the bar and hurried upstairs, Pomp took notice. Folding an excellent hand, he excused himself and went up the stairs.

When he opened the door to Abby's room unannounced, Rummy was holding a silk chemise to the sobbing whore's left ear.

Rummy spun about, protest dying on his lips.

When Abby saw Pomp she began crying harder. She made straight for him, causing Rummy to skitter along beside her in an attempt to keep the chemise against her ear. She threw her arms about Pomp. The three of them stood closer than they ever had before.

Pomp gently took Rummy's hand away and the sallow barkeep stepped aside.

Pomp examined the wound. The knife had cleanly sliced off the upper tip of ear.

Abby's gasps spewed heat into Pomp's ear.

"He used my best chemise!"

She shot a withering glance at the wilting barkeep.

"I'm so sorry, Abby. Really, I didn't know what to do. You are bleeding. It was the first thing I saw."

"It cost me a half week's measly salary."

"I'm certain he'll reimburse you," said Pomp.

Rummy's eyes sparked.

"I certainly will not," he said.

Pomp regarded him.

"And I am certain you will."

Rummy held out his hands.

"I was only trying to help."

"And you did, quite splendidly," said Pomp, examining the ear. "The bleeding has nearly stopped. Does it hurt much?"

"Not much," said Abby, wiping a cheek with the clean end of the chemise. "The pain is to my wardrobe and my pride."

Pomp's eyes swung about the room. Everything remained tidily placed.

"What happened?"

"He requested something I refused to do. He thought the knife would persuade me. When it didn't, he took off a piece of my ear. It happened so fast."

Abby's ear was beginning to trickle blood and she was starting to huff again.

Pomp turned to Rummy.

"Bring her a bottle of your best whisky, ice and several pieces of clean cloth. She applies the whisky, you apply the cloth and ice." He gave the barkeep a meaningful look. "Your *best* whisky. Not the horse urine that's left a bad taste in my mouth."

After Rummy left Pomp said, "I don't suppose he told you his vessel."

"No."

"I'd better go."

"He is still downstairs?"

"Last I looked."

When Pomp reached the door Abby said, "Thank you."

"It will be my pleasure."

The whaler was leaving as Pomp came downstairs, plucking a new bowler from the hat rack by the door. Pomp knew the bowler did not belong to the man.

Pomp mounted the white mare. Following the whaler was easy. The man staggered magnificently as he proceeded down Bradford Street. He didn't turn around. Arrogance was many a man's Achilles heel.

When the whaler turned down one of the alleys leading to Provincetown harbor, Pomp dismounted. Touching the mare's muzzle gently, he left her. No one in their right mind would approach a horse her size.

Pomp caught up with the man halfway down the alley.

Across the black water the rigging of a whaling ship rose into the night sky.

"Bid farewell to your ship."

To his credit, the man wheeled quicker than any drunk should, the knife already in his hand.

First Pomp used the cudgel to break the man's wrist.

The man fell to his knees.

Pomp kicked the knife away.

"Bastard," the man said.

"How did you know?" Pomp said, gently rapping the man's skull.

Bending, he picked up the bowler and placed it on his head.

An old man stood at the entrance to the alley. He had eyes like a fish. Pomp did not miss how the eyes grew even larger when the man saw his face.

Pomp tapped the rump of the man draped over his shoulder.

"Another victim of grog," Pomp said, settling the limp whaler across the horse.

Icarus snorted but she did back away. The mare knew the scent of blood.

The old man still stared.

Swinging up into the saddle, Pomp spoke to Icarus.

"Not all require the stupefying effects of alcohol," he said.

The moon was full. Squatting on a rise beside the marsh, Pomp whittled and, between the whaler's pleas, listened to the night. It was a lovely evening, an odd crispness marbling the air. Insects performed their singsong chants. The marsh grass, silver-gray in the moonlight, stood still, but the waters were already on the move.

On this rare night Pomp relished the moon

Three sandpipers picked their way daintily across the mud, circling the man buried to his neck. Finally the most brazen bird hopped forward and pecked the whaler's head.

For the first hour the man had shouted continuously. Pomp had marveled at his stamina. Then, having ascertained that the marsh was far removed from human ears, he had begun to plead.

Now his voice was cracked and ruined. Pomp had to lean forward to hear.

"Please. Let me go."

The whaler was a man of the sea. Pomp did not need to explain things to him. Already small rivulets of water ran across the mud. One bumped against the man's chin, wobbled, then passed along the left edge of his jaw, following the path of least resistance.

Water knew its way.

The man was different now. The predator was gone, replaced by something quivering and exposed upon a reeking field of mud.

Pomp watched the ash peel beneath the knife, rising up like a curling wave. He had taken up whittling during his own whaling days. It was now something of an obsession. It also kept his hand sharp.

"Mother of God. You can't do this."

The mud produced a queer half echo, which it promptly absorbed.

Pomp closed his eyes, enjoying the fine movements of the muscles in his hands. Hands were a remarkable tool, capable of anything.

Opening his eyes, he brushed a flake from his knee and spoke to the man and the cool night.

"We are an animal at odds. Michelangelo creates the Sistine Chapel; brother strangles brother at Vicksburg. Most men and women control their darker impulses, maybe by strength of will, but more likely for fear of society's retribution. But there will always be those who live without the fetters that stay the masses, men and women who lend no credence to the boundaries of civilization, whose only allegiance is to the whispers inside their head." The whaler could not turn his head, so Pomp regarded his profile. "I believe you understand."

"I'll give you anything."

"If you could, I believe you would."

Pomp rose from his crouch. Beneath his feet the marsh sucked and gave off fresh mud smell.

It was more needle than knife, but the blade still threw back the moonlight

The man panted like a wild dog.

His eyes darted about as his head could not.

"I'll give you anything. What do you want?"

"I do require something from you."

Crouching, Pomp took the proper token.

The noise saw the sandpipers take flight.

When he finished screaming, the whaler's chin fell to the mud.

The rivulets coalesced now, paper-thin pools jiggling in the moonlight. The whaler again raised his chin as high as he could. Now in the shadows, his head looked like an odd stump. No surprise to either man, the tide advanced quickly on the swollen moon.

The whaler began to soundlessly cry.

A sandpiper danced in and pecked at the smear where the ear had been.

Ten minutes later the whaler choked for the first time.

The moon watched. The tide rose.

The choking stopped.

It was late, but the encounter with the whaler had proved enervating and Pomp was wide awake. Instead of returning to his cabin in the Provincelands, he wandered the edge of the high cliffs that descended to the outer beach.

He had chosen to build his cabin in the Provincelands for a number of practical reasons, but the sheer beauty of the Provincelands had played a role too. On this summer night, the Outer Cape preened like a pageant queen. To the west, the towering dunes rose and fell like dusky swells on a frozen sea. Far below, the beach was nearly day-bright and moonlight spackled the sea. The waves, dark creases, rolled in, a silent, never-retreating army. As each wave neared shore, it gathered the moonlight on its rising face, sequined and sparkling.

A cool wind blew, touching Pomp's cheek like a mother's approving kiss. Not that he would know. His Negro mother had been a ship captain's maid; his father a Wampanoag Indian. Nature had frowned on the union, spitting him out into the world, unsightly and bent. His mother died within the hour. He had never seen his father. Raised in an orphanage, he had endured years of beatings at the hands of bullies and misfit staff until he put an end to it.

Walking the ridgeline, Pomp rocked as a ship rocks, for his legs were sorely bowed and the mild hump of his back saw him lean forward slightly, in turn causing his arms to swing. The motions made him look even more like an ape, but these days he allowed it to be so. He had dwelled with ugliness for thirty years, long enough to realize there was no changing it. But ugliness did not preclude a touch of style. Reaching up he ran an appreciative finger along the brim of the showroom soft bowler. The thought of it perched atop his head added bounce to his already jaunty step. It had been quite a night, filled with sweet revenge and good cards. The roll of bills pressed against his thigh. Not that he cared much for money. He had already amassed more wealth than most men saw in a lifetime, and there was always more on the way.

Even the scaffolding of the Peaked Hill Bars station didn't depress him. Rounding a dune, he came upon the station suddenly. It rose up into the night, scaffold signpost for a new world.

He stood for a time considering the outline of the two story structure. Soon enough it would be manned with surfmen, scurrying dutifully about. That Daniel Cole had been appointed Keeper would see these particular surfmen scurry even faster. Without doubt, they would be a detriment to his enterprise.

Standing beneath the heavens, the smile came to him slowly. The framework of the station resembled a skeleton.

This too shall pass.

In the interim, he was assembling the puzzle pieces he required. Soon enough a fresh approach would be in place and it would be up to the lifesavers to do what they could.

Crouching beside a beam, Pomp took out his knife. He had carved the mark hundreds of times. Still he worked carefully. When he finished, he wiped the wood flakes from the blade and left. Proceeding northwest, he followed the path that wound through the Provincelands to Provincetown. But he did not proceed to town. At a point familiar only to his eye, he left the path and vanished into the dunes.

The next morning when a carpenter bent to nailing, he stopped to run his finger around the perfect circle. He thought about calling the foreman over, but time was short and he had much to do.

He started hammering, one eye still on the circle that looked like an enlarged coin.

Or a full moon.

Rummy delivered the gift-wrapped box, addressed to Abby, two days later, stepping cautiously into Abby's room.

"It was on the bar when I opened," he said. "Do you have any idea how it got there?"

"No. And you still owe me a chemise."

Her ear had not stopped throbbing. It stripped her of her normally cheery demeanor.

She took the box from the barkeep's bony hand.

"I'm glad your customers appreciate you," Rummy said, but she had already turned her back to him.

She waited until the door shut. Opening the box, she smiled for the first time. She was not squeamish.

She would see to it that her knight in shining armor received fine reward.

# 4 TALES

Willie was wrong. All nine stations were completed by the end of August. By the middle of September they were manned and operating, the lifesavers patrolling Cape Cod's shoreline in shifts from sunset until dawn, and standing ready to respond twenty-four hours a day.

On September twenty-third the Chatham station responded to fall's first shipwreck, rowing out to a schooner shoved rudely on to the outer bar by unruly waves and winds. A commercial vessel ferrying lumber, all hands were rescued without a scratch and the ship was hauled off the bar when the winds calmed the following day. Washington, quick to claim glory, proclaimed the Cape safe for shipping. Two weeks later off Monomoy two lifesavers drowned when panicked passengers, lowered into the surfboat from a grounded packet boat, grabbed the surfmen, preventing them from rowing. Turned broadside to the waves, the surfboat flipped, depositing everyone in the sea. The passengers in the surfboat, and those aboard the packet boat hoping for rescue, all perished. Washington was quiet.

A week before Thanksgiving, a raging storm dismantled a packet boat ferrying travelers from New York to Boston. The ship went down in minutes, leaving baggage and praying, panting passengers and crew foundering in the heaving seas. Only one, outside the unfortunate, witnessed the ship's end. That evening a Race Point surfman patrolling the beach came upon an elderly couple at the foot of the great cliffs. How the woman had crawled there, the surfman couldn't guess. Her torso was laid open from breastplate to navel. The man beside her was unmarked, as if he had simply lain down to nap in his Sunday finery. When the surfman nudged the man with his boot, the man came alive with instant and alarming vigor, scuttling backward on his elbows and kicking out with his feet. The effort was his last.

The surfman had never seen such terror in a man's eyes, but when he returned to the station and reported the incident to his Keeper, the

Keeper only chuckled.

"No telling what a man's last nightmare might be," said John Kilbride.

The surfman came from a long line of farmers, growing cranberries in the bogs outside Harwich. Until now he had led a quiet, mosquito-plagued life, without violence. The vision of the woman rode roughshod in his head.

"Terrible sir, how the poor lady was sliced open by wreckage. I hope she didn't suffer."

"Only she knows."

John Kilbride was not a man who welcomed questioning, but the lifesaver was a God-fearing man.

"What about the bodies, sir? Shall I fetch the wagon?"

"No. Have the next patrol drag them to the water's edge," said John Kilbride, already walking away.

"But they were finely dressed sir. They're from wealth."

Kilbride turned slowly.

The surfman forgot about God.

"Let the tide take them and what remains of their worldly belongings," John Kilbride said.

It wasn't until the next morning, relieving himself against the side of the station, that the thought struck the surfman.

Queer that such a wealthy pair had sported no jewelry.

When Salem Wyman came to her room, at first Abby thought the fidgeting girl was going to ask for money. Abby Hierdal edged toward plump, but she kept her blond hair in ringlets and the way she moved made her the favorite of many men.

Salem entered the room with downcast eyes, but the moment the girl's bottom touched the chair, the eyes snapped wide.

"You're Pomp's friend," the girl blurted.

Abby tried to hide her surprise, although she was nearly certain Salem Wyman had no hidden motive. Abby barely knew the girl, Rummy had only hired her four months earlier, but she liked her for her gay laugh and spontaneous manner. She was so young, just turned sixteen, and seemingly unaware that guile and subterfuge existed. But Abby knew much of guile and subterfuge and so she was careful.

"He's my friend, yes."

"You've *slept* with him?"

Sleep was the last word to describe it.

"I have."

The girl leaned so far forward Abby thought she would topple from the chair.

"How is it?" Salem whispered. "I mean, he's got that hump. And he's so bowlegged and he looks like an ape."

"He is the most satisfying lover I've ever had."

It was the truth, and now she was having fun too.

"No!" The girl lost her last shred of shyness. "How? Is he *endowed*?"

"Amply enough. But more important, he understands women."

"Oh."

That the girl was only just beginning to understand herself was so obvious Abby had to swallow her smile. Abby noticed now that Salem had barely begun to develop breasts, although she had the legs of a fawn.

"What does he do?"

"Many things," said Abby.

"What kind of things?"

"Pleasant things, ruined by description."

This time Abby correctly guessed the question.

"Do you think he would sleep with me?"

"You are employed in a place where that can be arranged."

"But he has to ask for *me*."

Her desire was so honest Abby nearly dropped her guard.

"I was told an awful story," Salem said.

Again Abby was reminded that man was not a book to be casually paged through.

Only a clock's ticking occupied the room.

"You could tell me the story," said Abby helpfully.

"It's awful."

Abby knew the girl was not being coy.

"Not all stories are true," she said.

"This one is."

"How can you be so certain?"

"I laid with a man who saw it happen. When we finished, he told me the story."

"Saw what happen?"

The girl suddenly sat bolt upright, as if someone had just rung a bell only she could hear.

"Do you have tea?"

Abby had forgotten how it was to be sixteen.

"I do, and I'll fix some."

"Maybe with a little honey?"

"Of course."

While Abby readied the tea, Salem wandered about the room. Abby liked the way she touched things lightly and respectfully and put them carefully back in place.

"You have so many nice things."

Abby set the tea cups on the table.

"Most of them were gifts."

"From your men."

"From my men."

"The men I've been with haven't given me anything but a rash."

Abby's abilities had earned her certain customers of power and means. These influential customers she entertained elsewhere, away from prying eyes. Powerful men had equally powerful wives.

"Time will change that, Salem," she said kindly.

The flat-chested girl sipped her tea and beamed.

"Perfectly sweet! My mother makes the best tea, but yours is really good. Thank you."

"My pleasure. The story?"

The girl's face collapsed.

"It's horrid."

"It's the reason you came to my room."

The girl didn't even look surprised.

"I suppose it is," she said.

She told the story in a dull monotone, as if that would ease the unfolding. How the whaling ship went down suddenly in a squall off the Cook Islands, and those that were quick enough took to the whaleboats, four boats in all. How Pomp, who was the first mate, and the ship's captain ended up in the same whaleboat and, in the chaos of boarding, the captain's leg was crushed between the whaleboat and the ship. How the five men in Pomp's whaleboat finished the last of the hardtack on the fifth day and the last of the water two days later. How on the eighth day, the captain fell into delirium. With that, command of the boat fell to Pomp.

That night, he ordered the men to row away from the other boats. The other men protested, but they were weak and somehow Pomp was not. That first night the three whalers huddled in the stern, fists in their ears, as the anguished screams rolled over the dark water. Eventually the screaming dwindled away, replaced by a queer gurgling.

The girl's face was drawn; creases furrowed her brow. It was as if the tale was sucking the youth from her before Abby's eyes.

"At dawn, Pomp covered the captain's body with a tarp. They drifted for two more days and nights. The three whalers stayed huddled in the stern. At night they shouted prayers, but they still heard the tarp rustle."

The girl's eyes fixed on the far wall, as if the whaleboat was rowing toward them.

"A ship found them. Their rescuers hoisted the whaleboat up to the deck and a sailor pulled back the tarp. Both calves were gone, and so was most of the fat on the legs. Pomp had applied tourniquets. When the sailors lifted the body, the captain sighed."

A sudden banging erupted from the room next door. A minute later a man cried out.

Neither woman heard. The girl's eyes remained fixed on some faraway place.

"There was an inquiry, but the other whalers wouldn't speak. That a man would go so far and that other men would allow it."

Abby knew the story, just as she knew what turned the girl throaty.

Power was an elixir.

Pomp came to her that night, rendering her sensual and senseless.

When they finished, he left the bed.

Slipping back beside her, he said, "A small gift."

The box was long and thin.

She wondered if she had ever been so content.

She turned the box slowly.

"Is it fragile?"

"Not overly."

"I love a mystery."

"Initially it was a mystery to me."

The silver chain was lovely, but the sapphire pendant was lovelier still.

He had given her gifts before, but nothing like this.

"It's breathtaking," she said.

"As are you."

For an instant she wished he wasn't so ugly. She hoped he didn't see it in her face. She was glad for the darkness.

"Darkness is my friend," he said softly and her skin chilled.

She lay quiet; again, her heart raced.

After a moment, Pomp said, "It turned out to be quite the well. I also retrieved a pair of earrings, a gold wedding band and a man's stick pin, pearls set in gold. That one must have provided some difficulty."

Pomp rolled on to his back. From the corner of her eye, she watched his simian profile stare up at the ceiling.

"Not everyone in the audience enjoyed my fishing about." He spoke softly. "Ironic, isn't it? A woman who refuses to swallow her husband's ejaculate will, upon the deck of a sinking ship, choke down a platter's worth of jewels. Mankind bestows me with ceaseless puzzles and lessons."

He rolled back to face her. The alert eyes seemed to radiate a heat she felt on her face. Not once had she seen him tired. He was always alive to the world.

She kissed him. His lips were rough.

"I love the way you live," she whispered.

"I love the way you love. It is no puzzle why grown men spill their secrets to you."

She didn't want to think of the other men now.

"You could have others," she said.

"For now you will do."

Salem's fawn legs moved languidly before her eyes. She decided to never mention the girl.

"I'd run off with you this instant," she said.

Pomp chuckled.

"We have too much to do here. The great dull weight of the sheep threatens all that we love."

All that *you* love. She tried to stifle the thought.

"Not all progress is bad," she said.

"No? I confess I am still searching for the gems bestowed by your purported progress. Perhaps the lifesaving stations are among them."

She heard the edge in his voice.

"We have John Kilbride with us," she said.

"We do. But he is only one man, albeit a large and appreciably violent one."

"They are only men. Monomoy has already proven that."

"Some of them were good men," Pomp said. "The sea does not recognize good or evil, fool or genius, man or child. The dispassionate waters seize them all."

Outside the wind rose.

Abby knew the stations worried Pomp. The Monomoy incident had proved the lifesavers fallible, but they both knew the lifesaving stations would make their work far more difficult.

"Daniel Cole."

Pomp spoke the man's name as if he had just entered the room. It startled her, and being startled made her a trifle angry.

"What about him?"

"Do you know him?"

"I know of him. I know he is now Keeper at Peaked Hill Bars. He came here with his wife. He spoke with Willie Bangs."

"I know," said Pomp, and there was a touch of sadness in his voice. "And what do you hear of Daniel Cole?"

"That he is quiet and capable." She kicked herself for saying it. "A good fisherman and husband, but no more than an average man who will dissolve into the sands of time."

The bed creaked.

Pomp went to the window.

"I saw him once in a fight. It started as just a fight between boys, but it did not end that way."

"What happened?"

"Daniel Cole knocked the other boy down with a man's punch. It was over to everyone except Daniel Cole. He fell on the boy. It took four of us to drag him off."

"That seems common enough."

"Not to those of us who saw him trying to rip the boy's throat out."

They both thought about this.

"What were they fighting about?" Abby asked.

"A girl named Nellie Paine. The boy on the wrong end of the beating called her a whore."

Abby did not miss the jibe or how it stung.

"He intrigues and troubles me," said Pomp.

"He is only one man."

Pomp did not smile.

"That remains to be seen," he said.

# 5 SECRETS

Pomp visited Marmaduke Matthews on a blustery Sunday night two weeks before Christmas. The minister's cottage sat at the top of a hill behind the Presbyterian Church, reached by a short, but steep, brick path. Between cold gusts, Pomp heard the labored breathing of the woman beside him.

Pomp didn't knock. He went in alone, padding soundlessly down the long entry to the only lit room.

Reverend Matthews sat in an armchair before a blazing fire. Apparently the scarcity of wood on the Cape was of no concern here.

"You have a visitor."

Marmaduke Matthews stood and spun in one quick motion.  For a fat man he was surprisingly quick. He was wearing silk pajamas.

The expression on the Reverend's face was clear.

"I am sorry to disappoint you," said Pomp.

The minister regained his composure with equivalent speed.

"No disappointment at all. I am just accustomed to people knocking."

"You are readying for bed?"

Marmaduke Matthews walked to a cabinet across the room.

"Actually, I was just about to have a whisky." They both knew it was a lie. "Care to join me?"

"Yes."

The Reverend motioned to the fire.

"Please. Take the other chair."

Pomp sat. The fire threatened to scorch off his eyebrows. He pushed his chair back. An end table sat beside the minister's chair. A half completed chess game rested on the table.

Marmaduke brought the whisky.

"I play against myself," he said, handing Pomp a tumbler and settling into his own chair.

"Do you prove a worthy adversary?"

"More often than I like."

"Good. I have come to discuss a thinking man's game."

It was a simple plan. There was a certain risk in divulging it to the minister, but Pomp had already dropped one hook in the water and the minister had readily gobbled it up. The man no longer sat on the right hand of God.

Pomp explained things quickly.

The minister stared into the fire. Pomp saw how the man did not have the courage to meet his eyes, yet still he played his own game.

"Mooncussing is illegal," Marmaduke Matthews said.

"I prefer to think of myself as an opportunistic wrecker."

"The local constabulary won't see it that way."

"The local constabulary will never see it."

"How can you be so sure?"

"Because I have been practicing it now for almost ten years."

Marmaduke Matthews absorbed this. Ships falsely lured ashore. Men, women and children brought to their death. Even with the plunder involved, it saw him hesitate.

He failed at sounding casual.

"How often?"

"When weather and sea cooperate."

The ocean terrified Marmaduke Matthews. Once, as a boy, he had stood with others on a winter beach, watching helplessly as a schooner met its end. The ship had grounded on a shoal no more than seventy yards from shore. Holding his mother's hand he had watched as sailors and passengers fell screaming from the deck and rigging, the ocean swallowing their final sound. The sand had stung his face like bird shot. He had nightmares for months, crying souls sweeping past him, their arms outstretched.

He reminded himself that he was now a grown man.

"Are others involved in this enterprise?" he asked.

"You need only be concerned with your part."

"It is quite a risk for me."

"It is a risk for all of us."

"And what might I expect in return?"

"A degree of remuneration."

"Irregular remuneration."

"I will make it as regular as possible."

As a minister Marmaduke Matthews had his own substantial network of sources, yet not once had he heard a whisper of mooncussing.

*Almost ten years.*

"You have already collected... things?"

The laugh was a bark.

"Yes."

There was no fear in the minister's eyes now.

"What manner of things?"

"It has been rewarding." Pomp reached into his jacket pocket, extricating a leather pouch. "You cannot imagine the gifts bequeathed by the spectrum of mankind."

Greed made people look like pigs, a shorter step in the case of the jowly minister.

"For me?"

"A small advance against risk."

"May I open it?"

"I'd hoped you would."

The fat fingers fumbled with the drawstring, but they found their way through the opening quickly enough.

Pomp heard the intake of breath.

The hook was set. He gave it a final tug.

"It is one in a matching pair."

"It's pure gold?"

"It is."

Their chess game was over.

The minister surprised him.

"What about the surf lifesavers?"

"They do not concern you. You just undertake what I ask."

"You ask me to violate the trust of my parishioners." Both men knew this didn't matter. "I am exposing myself to substantial risk. If I am unearthed it will be the end of me."

"Yes it will."

Pomp laid a finger atop the king.

"Some say it is what separates us from the beasts."

"What?"

Pomp's eyes went to the hearth.

"Fire," he said.

"I suppose."

Pomp considered the flames.

"I am not yet convinced we are separate."

"We are distinct from the beasts," the minister said. "Separated by soul and intellect."

"Of course. We have ably applied both to so many things."

The minister shifted.

"We have," he said.

"The Babylonians."

The fire crackled. A log fell, sending up sparks. Pomp gently rocked the king to and fro.

Marmaduke said, "What of them?"

"Mathematicians. Astronomers. Artisans and physicians. Far ahead of their time. They discovered that you can run a man through with a thousand sharp instruments without touching an organ of import. Of course they also believed that those who were not Babylonian were lesser breeds, and so, less sensitive to pain."

When Pomp stood, the king toppled.

"There are worse ends than unveiling."

Abby waited outside, a scowl beneath the hood.

"It took a bit longer than expected," Pomp said. "I am truly sorry."

"And I am truly frozen. Is he with us?"

"I believe we have won him over."

"Perfect."

"No. It is imperfection that serves us."

Reaching out, Pomp gently took a windblown ringlet between two fingers.

"I appreciate this," he said.

"I know."

He let the ringlet fall.

"I suspect he is a trifle less eager than usual, but I have no doubt you will remedy that quickly enough."

That night in his cabin Pomp allowed himself a small celebration. He cooked mutton, accompanying it with a bottle of his best whisky. The minister was the last puzzle piece. It was a simple triumvirate. Abby would relay the confidences of clients, men who knew the ships' schedules and their cargoes. The oily minister would glean similar confidences, for the same men who slept with a whore, knelt in a pew. Apprised of what would pass along their shores, they could only hope for Nature's cooperation. But Nature had cooperated with untoward zeal since man raised his first sail upon the sea. When storm and ship coincided, he and John Kilbride would see to the rest.

The minister was right. He had divulged more than enough to jeopardize his position. But now they both knew the minister would take their shared secret to the grave. And only a fool divulged everything. The whore, the Keeper and the minister knew only what they needed to know.

Oh yes, there were other secrets. Buried everywhere. And more to come. He was only just beginning.

The voice in the dark cabin did not sound like his.

"That life is long, which answers life's great end. The rise of the mooncusser."

Pomp tipped back the tumbler, the warmth of the whisky and the smile coming to him in equally languid time.

He did not eat all the mutton. He did not approve of gluttony. When he finished, he placed the leftovers on a tin plate and went outside.

Stepping from the listing porch to the sand, he stood for a moment enjoying the rightness of his chosen home. A host of stars winked overhead. The silent dunes reached up, trying to touch them.

Placing the plate in the sand, Pomp returned to the porch and sat in the rocker.

He did not have to wait long. They arrived like ghosts. Padding across the sand, they cast sidelong glances his way. There were three of them. The smallest, a young pup, whimpered and yelped before charging incautiously to the plate. The pup gobbled what it could before the snarling parents shoved it aside.

When the mutton was gone the adults turned and left, melding first into darkness and then into the dunes.

The pup did not leave. It stood alone beneath the stars, legs splayed in the fashion of a newborn deer, staring at the porch. It was oddly brazen behavior for a young pup.

Pomp lifted his tumbler in salute.

The pup did not require his approval. Gathering its legs, the wild dog flowed easily across the sand and disappeared.

# 6 THE STORM

John Kilbride ruptured with unrest. He recognized it, even as it welled up inside him. The fits had assumed him since he was a boy. As a boy he had drained them with his fists. As a man he had other options.

He didn't know why the energy rose up in him, massing and churning and pressing until he wanted to tear his way out of his own skin. But it did.

He spoke to William Cook, seated at the table near the kitchen.

"I'm leaving."

William Cook was nearly as large as Kilbride. A truculent man in the best of times, on this particular evening Cook possessed an even darker mood, being charged with supper duty.

"One less for supper," he muttered.

William Cook did not look up from his cards. His opponent, a skinny boy named Jon Enoch, coughed uncomfortably.

In any other man this would be insubordination, but Kilbride hadn't hired William Cook for his manners. Still a certain degree of authority had to be maintained.

Kilbride laughed.

"I'd be mad to eat whatever it is you plan to prepare," he said, and just as quickly his voice went cold. "You would do well to look at me. You should also ask where I am going."

William Cook looked up.

"Where are you going?"

"Provincetown."

"It's preparing to storm."

"Oh yes it is," Kilbride said, and the skinny boy looked down at his feet. It had only been six months, but Kilbride was already long sorry he had hired the boy. He had done it as a favor to a friend. The boy had proved capable enough, but he possessed the manner of a woman. Kilbride saw the boy's eyes questioning his every decision. They questioned him now.

"Something to say, Surfman Enoch?"

To his credit, the boy looked up from his feet.

"The patrols haven't been assigned," he said quietly.

Race Point Station sat between Wood End Station near the mouth of Provincetown Harbor and Peaked Hill Bars, three miles down the outer beach to the southeast. Each night, in three shifts, two surfmen left the station to patrol, one walking toward Peaked Hill Bars, the other toward Wood End. Halfway between the stations they met with the surfman from the other station. Exchanging a metal token to mark their meeting, each surfman turned back for his respective station.

His men neglected plenty of their duties, but if they didn't patrol Washington would hear of it quickly. Kilbride did not want Washington nosing about in his business.

"You'll take the first patrol and the last," he said to the boy.

The boy was smart. He kept his tongue.

"You will assign the other patrols, Mr. Cook. Do not neglect to include yourself among them."

Kilbride saw the anger in the big man's face, but he had no more time for him. The storm he knew so well was kicking against his insides.

Taking his coat from the hook beside the door, he plunged out into the night where the sleet was just beginning.

Salem Wyman was glad for the sleet pelting her window with a gritty hiss. It would keep business away. She wasn't in the mood for business. Stormy nights made her sad. She missed her family. She had run away from Philadelphia to make an adventure of her life. Sitting in this small room that always smelled of rubbing alcohol to push away the other smells, she saw where her adventure had ended.

The man didn't knock. He was simply there, filling the entire doorway, breathing fast. There were no preliminaries. She felt herself yanked up like a doll and crushed against the wall and there was pain and panicked breathing, hers or his she couldn't tell. Her body no longer belonged to her. She twisted and jerked about. Twice her head hit the wall so hard she nearly blacked out. She wished for unconsciousness, but some instinct told her that blacking out would only make things worse. She had been treated roughly before, but never like this. She screamed silently until the thrusting man sagged.

He placed the money on the bed and left without a word.

She felt stickiness between her legs and on the back of her head. The stickiness on the back of her head was still spreading. She knew she should have someone look at it. Instead she thought of her bed in Philadelphia, with its perfumy pillows and the colorful afghan her mother had knitted for her.

She rocked herself and cried.

Her neck felt queer and something rolled loosely in her head.

She remembered a man, stronger than the man who had brutalized her. It gave her courage.

She tried to remember the man she wanted to meet but she couldn't.

She cried again.

The sleet had turned to snow. When John Kilbride stepped from the Cork and Barrel, a horse and rider waited. The rider displayed yellow teeth.

"I feel a change in the weather," said Pomp.

It was bitter cold on Bradford Street, but it was far colder atop the high dune cliffs. Racing off the sea, wind and snow raked the two men and the great white horse walking the ridgeline.

It was a cold like steel laid to bone.

Neither man nor beast felt the cold. The horse was occupied with animal thoughts; the strain of the wagon, the queer shudderings of anticipation. The men searched the dark, heaving seas; curtains of snow and foam torn from whitecaps making a sail nearly impossible to see.

Hanging from the horse's neck, the swaying lantern produced a foggy glow.

The wind's howling made talk difficult. Kilbride was glad. He did not feel like talking. He walked the ridgeline, slushy sand beneath his feet, enjoying the crackling, like a constant lightning strike, coursing through his body. The taking of the whore had filled him with his power, reminding him of who he was.

It felt as good to conquer a woman as it did to cripple a man. The young whore had bounced about like a willing rag doll. He would visit her again.

The hand gripped his elbow with a force that saw him wince with pain.

The ape beside him had already let go.

Pomp pointed to the northeast.

At first Kilbride saw nothing but black sea and white night. Slowly, the sails that remained morphed out of the snow.

The ship looked like a child's toy, but it was no child's game. Even from this distance Kilbride could see the vessel pitching wildly. The captain had already ordered down most of the sails. Kilbride did not need to be on the deck to know that a world was crumbling: splintering, rending, fraying and unraveling beneath the thunderous slatting of the canvas that remained.

As they watched the mainmast dipped precipitously, as if desperately trying to snatch something from the leaping seas.

Pomp gave the swaying lantern a nudge.

The captain of the vessel proved supremely capable. With barely any sail, and most of that shredded, he navigated his ship amidst waves exploding upon the shoals. Finding a channel between bars he made for the swaying light, heaven sent miracle. Perhaps his crew was cheering until the uninterrupted spread of shore hove into view and the keel drove headlong into the sand.

Some were brained by falling timbers. Others, pitched overboard by the sudden halt, were smashed against the ship by the waves, their insides broken to pieces. Some drowned, wrapped in rigging. Some drowned, unable to swim twenty yards through crashing walls of frigid water.

Pomp doused the lantern and the two men waited. After an hour they made their way to where the path descended from the cliffs to the beach.

There they waited again. If there were survivors, it was best to allow them time to make their way inland.

Checking his pocket watch, Pomp again saw that the timing had been perfect. The patrolling surfmen would not pass for at least two hours. It was too dangerous to board the vessel now, but should the seas settle slightly he had no qualms about boarding in the dark. In that case, Kilbride could help. Otherwise the Keeper would have to leave before dawn. But he could stay. When dawn came, he could be accused of nothing but uncanny prescience. Should the other wreckers arrive before he could board, he did not mind sharing.

Pomp smiled. It was really the simplest of exercises. A lantern or two displayed from the high ridgeline, a desperate captain, blinded by snow, sleet, or fog, who might mistake the swaying lantern for a ship at anchor and make for safe harbor.

He forced no one ashore. It wasn't even coercion. Their fate was in their own hands, as a man's fate should be.

The snow thinned. The wind eased. As if Nature saw her job was complete.

Pomp said silent thanks and, with a click of the reins, guided the wagon down to the beach.

They found the man halfway up the beach. He was dark-skinned and curled about himself. He straightened when Pomp crouched beside him.

"What ails you?"

The man's eyes wandered and then focused. His pupils were black as olives.

"Something inside me is broken."

"Is it painful?"

"It will pass."

"Are you mulatto?"

"I am Kiowa Apache."

"A race of tenacity and fight."

"So it is said."

"My father was Wampanoag."

The man winced.

"A poor time to be any manner of Indian. We held ourselves invincible. Now our end is near. Beware arrogance."

The man's eyes went to Kilbride standing beside the wagon. The Indian watched him thoughtfully and then he began to cough violently.

Turning his head to the sand, he emptied his mouth of blood.

"I know what you men did," he said.

Pomp nodded.

"How does a Kiowa Apache come to be so far from home?"

"I wished for an untamed place."

The snow had stopped and a heavier cold had descended, as if someone had pulled away a blanket.

The man lay on his side, blood leaking from his mouth. He closed his eyes.

Kilbride started to speak, but Pomp raised a hand.

After a time, the man opened his eyes.

"I prefer the desert heat."

"I am sorry for what has happened. Would you like whisky?"

"It would be wasted."

The man suffered another fit of coughing. Blood splattered.

Pomp took a cloth from his pocket and wiped the man's face.

"Do you wish for help?"

"I walked my own path. I wish to finish in the same manner."

He went quiet again, though his eyes remained open.

In the darkness the sea thundered.

Kilbride said, "The patrols will pass by soon."

"I am unconcerned."

The three men waited until only two were waiting.

Pomp stood. Everyone looked smaller in death.

"The sea is the last wild place."

John Kilbride watched the humped figure drag the body down to the riotous water.


AND SO IT CONTINUES...

# FOG

## 1  BEGINNINGS AND ENDINGS

They ran across the sloping deck like marionettes, arms and legs akimbo, and when the waves caught the sailors, their arms jerked out, snatching at the night, before they disappeared without a sound.

The rude cold filched her breath. When the waves rushed toward her, foaming and leaping and rumbling across the deck faster than any man could run—she knew this now— she drew what breath she could and felt her body clench. The waves carried their own wicked cold, so cold it burned, but the fizzing blackness they brought was worse, shutting her away in the darkest loneliness on earth. She believed in God. She prayed for the time between the waves, when the wind screamed and the snow made angry locust clicks but the stars hung peacefully and were still. She imagined the stars were angels, waiting.

She supposed she might not die. Father had tied her to the mainmast, carefully folding her arms across her chest. The rope had cut into her, although she no longer felt its bite. She had watched his hands proudly, the beautiful fingers expertly cinching the knots, but there was something different in his face. Mother had believed in God, but Father trusted no one, not even God, and when he finished his tying, he fell against her and pushed his lips to her ear and told her to keep her secret close and fight for her life. He prayed a lie, promising God he would do anything if he gave her safe passage, and then asked her to forgive him for what he had done to her. She accepted everything, kissing his eyelids, and when the waves swallowed them she felt his arms about her. Finally, a wave smothered them and, as if he didn't care anymore, he was gone, and she almost gave up.

Far above her, the last sailor regarded the red pinprick of lanterns on the shore and loosed his fingers from the icy rigging. He fell like a pinwheel in a faint breeze, and when he struck the *Asia's* deck, he gave an odd little hop. He was a quick-handed boy, marvelous at jacks, but now he lay twisted in an impossible shape, sliding down the deck to join the black waves lumbering to shore.

The great wave rose in the same way her friend had fallen, with queer slowness. It kept rising, gray front streaked with white, until she wondered if she was sinking. She said good-bye to the stars, closing her eyes and squeezing Miss Lolly to her chest.

The deck shuddered. She was swallowed again in iron cold. She felt herself tipping, the mainmast splintering away, and she was swept easily into the sea, riding for a moment as if on the softest mattress. And then she was spinning, turning over and over, her lungs screaming for air in roaring darkness that never gave way to show the stars.

She wanted to die, but she fought to live because Father wished it, and it was possible that God listened to everyone's prayers, even Father's.

On the beach, Captain Edwin Merton's agonies were many. His mistake had seen his ship, his crew, and his only child into the sea. The wave that had deposited him ashore had snapped four ribs and a femur. Crawling toward the great cliffs, he had felt the separations only as mild burning; cold and shock had served as anesthesia.

At the foot of the cliffs, he had lain for a time, confused. With all the sensations clamoring for his attention, it was difficult to concentrate on any one matter until the angel arrived, holding the reins of the great white horse. The angel had dissolved behind the passing curtains of white, so that at first Edwin Merton thought it a hallucination. But when the angel crouched beside him, the breath behind the brilliant smile was rancid. The knife sliding down his midsection brought a stench equally as real, and blood filled his mouth as he turned his cheek to the snowy sand.

The blade's deft workings brought him great focus. Yet even as he suffered agonies he had not thought possible, he recognized the justness of his punishment. He shouted agreement, raining oaths upon himself and powers that would see a child to such an end. The angel brushed his cheek tenderly with downy knuckles and spoke encouragement in his ear, lauding him for atoning for his sins, but it was only his daughter's voice he heard; after a pause, the angel returned to cutting. The angel was an artist, skirting the organs that sustain life, touching the places that chimed. There were partings, tuggings, burstings, sour nausea, regret. Snow caressed his organs. Lifting his head, he saw his body's warmth, a steamy wavering in the dark, not quite a soul.

The punishment was just, but the pain was too great. Captain Merton set his will against the knife. His will was strong, and his raging only aided his demise.

His end caused the angel a melodious sigh. Applying the knife carefully, the angel removed the organ that mattered. When he finished, he buried Captain Edwin Merton with the same precision that had ushered his end.

Hewing to nature's course, child outlived parent. Two miles south of Edwin Merton's grave, at the foot of the Cape Cod cliffs, Isabella Merton, spread upon the wooden table in the day house, looked up into a boy's eyes. The boy had sad eyes, but not so sad that Isabella forgot her own troubles.

After all her efforts, she was certain.

"I'm going to die," she said.

Above her, the boy kept staring, his mouth making strange motions. She thought of her father and the broken sailor, and her mother with her helpless eyes and phlegmy cough. Nothing could be done. This understanding brought a sleepy comfort.

"Don't be frightened," she said. "It can't be helped."

She pressed her chin to Miss Lolly's head, feeling the coarse wood where the hair, once flower-petal soft, had torn away. Everything grand, now ruined and spoiled.

"Miss Lolly and I were going to be the talk of New York," she whispered. "We were going to ride in a steam elevator. I hate the sea."

A kettle whistled merrily. She tried to keep thinking about the elevator, but her legs, which had only tingled at first, were warming. It was not a comfortable warming like the morning sun against your skin, but a fast-rising heat, as if she had stepped too close to a fire. When the big man drew back the canvas, she saw her legs and she knew something terrible was rushing up on her.

The big man had lied to her, although his lies, like his face, had been kind. She and the big man had played a game, pretending they hadn't seen the truth. The silent boy hadn't played. She liked the boy for not lying, nearly loved him for the way he looked at her as if they were best friends, but when he reached for Miss Lolly she had to scold him.

When the big man placed the handkerchief, rolled like a sausage, in her mouth, she closed her eyes and bit down hard, and her heart scampered.

There was a creaking, like a wagon wheel starting to turn. The pain was shocking. Almost as quickly, a deadening flowed over her. The black ocean, the fire in her legs, her faithful doll, they drifted away. The wooden table became her hilltop swing. As she rose and fell, the wind tickling her ears, she gazed again beyond the farthest edge of England's green fields, toward the grandest country in the world, a place where stalwart men and upright ladies dressed in the latest fashions and danced to music played on electric phonographs and rode in steam elevators, up, up, up, beyond the birds. It was sore disappointment to have sailed across the ocean to find instead an America so loud and foul-mannered. America didn't deserve her secret. She wasn't going to change the world. She was just going to die.

When dawn came, only the ocean raged, as the jagged remains of the *Asia* lay dark against the gray November sky.

# 2 BURIAL

The storm that saw to the *Asia's* end passed to the west. Ferocious cold pooled in its wake, gripping the Cape for a week. In Wellfleet, Chatham, and Provincetown harbors, the winter of 1882 cemented its already considerable reputation by crushing a dozen skipjacks in ice. In the marshes, jagged blocks of ice as big as men lay strewn about, and the creeks and channels shone milky white. Even Ezekiel Donne, who in all seasons walked about the dunes in his underthings, remained inside. At the Cape's far tip only the wild dogs padded through the Provincelands, moving like lethargic shadows.

On the eighth day, a wane sun appeared and the Peaked Hill Bars surfmen buried the *Asia's* dead. A steady wind blew from the northeast, jostling the smaller limbs of Provincetown Cemetery's lone oak, the sound like bones scraping.

The men had built a fire first, hoping to thaw the frozen ground, but it proved nearly fruitless.

"Better luck burrowing under a nun's knickers," said Willie Bangs, bouncing his shovel off the stubborn moraine.

Still, they proceeded with muted curses. Eight sailors, glazed with the same crust as the frozen earth, waited for their single grave. The girl lay in the beach cart twenty yards away. The cart was no more than a wood slab resting on spoked wheels; without sides, it allowed a clear view of the small pine coffin.

Daniel Cole frowned on delay and swearing. Captain Daniel Cole, keeper of Peaked Hill Bars Lifesaving Station, always insisted on a prompt burial, but weather and circumstance had forced a rare exception. The Atlantic had been slow in relinquishing the dead; burying made no sense until all the bodies were collected.

The *Asia's* crew washed ashore over the course of a week, the surfmen transporting the bodies to Peaked Hill Bars Lifesaving Station in the beach cart. Thoreau, the brown bay gelding, strained as the wheels slipped in the sand. The lifesavers stacked the bodies outside, cinching a canvas tarp tightly over the pile. The wild dogs normally kept to the Provinceland wilds, but winter's deprivations drove them farther afield.

On Captain Cole's order, the girl remained in the day house just away from the main station, her body packed in snow and wrapped in canvas. The corpse proved inconvenient. Resting near the edge of the high sand cliffs, the day house served as a lookout for ships in distress. The single room, with its potbellied stove, chair, and table, was already cramped, and although the girl was small, the table was smaller. Performing day watch, the surfmen had to move gingerly to avoid bumping the protruding canvas.

Each man handled the inconvenience in his fashion. Frank Mayo and the Swede, Martin Nelson, kept their backs to the corpse at all times; Mayo because he cared little about any death, save his own; Nelson in a doomed attempt to forget. Antone Lucas, the diminutive Azores islander, was consumed with avoiding his reflection in the windows: seeing one's reflection in the presence of a corpse was invitation to die next. Hedging his bets, he kept one hand jammed in his trousers pocket, squeezing a lucky acorn. Ben Maddocks prayed for the girl's soul. During his watch, Willie Bangs engaged the girl in amiable conversation; it was rare to pass time with someone who never interrupted. Cole relieved young Hiram Paine of day watch, a rare exception to duties executed to the letter.

Though the men were unhappy about digging, they were glad to be rid of the bodies.

Willie watched Captain Cole walk to the beach cart. As Cole bent to the coffin, Ornish Helms sidled toward the keeper. Provincetown's undertaker, Ornish Helms had supplied the pine box. There was no time to craft coffins for the sailors, and more pertinent, no one to pay for them. There had been no money for the girl's coffin either. Cole had had to summon his ample powers of persuasion to get Ornish to donate the girl's box.

The thin undertaker approached the cart slowly. It amused Willie that most people approached the keeper in the same wary fashion, as if engaging a mad dog or an irate spouse— not, in Willie's experience, that there was much difference.

But when Cole turned away from the coffin, Ornish Helms fairly leapt forward. The keeper stood still while the undertaker's hands danced in the air.

Willie rested his shovel against a weathered headstone and rubbed his wrists.

"No doubt lamenting another heinous financial slight resulting from his generous nature," he said. "Why we had to bury these men on a day when the ground is balkier than a deaf mule is beyond me. It's not like they were going to sit up and walk off in a huff if they weren't accommodated."

"They might walk off at the rate you're digging," said Frank Mayo.

Normally, Mayo enjoyed listening to Willie. The man's tongue was lively and its waggings produced amusement and distraction in a job that saw little of either. But Mayo's every joint ached, and Willie's desultory digging wasn't improving his mood.

"The dead could outshovel you and get us out of here sooner," Mayo added.

"They're welcome to up and lend a hand," said Willie, "though I doubt they share your concern with time."

The other men had stopped digging. They stood silent, displaying hangdog faces. Their dour mood made Willie's spirits rise.

"The rest of God's creatures appreciate the moment," he said. "I'd wager they even appreciate a day as miserable as this. But not man. Even in our happiest moments, we're rushing off somewhere else. What's our hurry?" His eyes swept the cemetery. "Here's what we're rushing to."

"Bad luck to speak of death," muttered Ben Maddocks, crossing himself and commencing to dig again.

"I don't know if you're paying attention, but I doubt our luck could turn much worse," said Willie. "But as these gentlemen would no doubt heartily attest, even the worst moments are worth living. Still, you have to step back and notice them. Keeping your eyes on the ground is fine work for cows and moles."

"Maybe you'd like to explain your philosophy of leisure to Captain Cole," said Mayo.

"God knows I've tried," said Willie, glancing toward the wagon. Ornish Helms was still waving his hands at the keeper. "The man isn't much for philosophy, as we all well know. He isn't much for any of the world's pleasures that I can tell."

"That would include an afternoon in your company," said Mayo, resuming his digging.

The rest of the men took up their digging too.

"You'd be surprised who enjoys a lengthy afternoon in my company," said Willie, snubbing his shovel. "You could start by asking some of the women you've courted."

Frank Mayo possessed tousled, wheat-colored hair and a like-hued mustache, lovingly tended. "The women I court might be interested in you as a museum piece," he said.

"Women enjoy an older man," Willie said. "He's more apt to pay attention to their needs, rather than his own reflection."

"You need to pay attention to digging, or we'll be burying these men in the dark."

Despite himself, Willie jumped. In ten years of service under Daniel Cole, Willie had never gotten used to the man's approach. He walked like a deer and, more annoying still, rarely announced himself. Had it been any other man, Willie would have sworn he was the butt of a subtly crafted joke.

Willie forgot his good mood. "I wish you'd quit walking like a wisp of fog. Man my age can't take too many starts."

"You won't die of overexertion," said Cole, taking up a shovel.

"I prefer to parcel my energy wisely."

"It would be wise to be gone from here before nightfall," said Cole.

"I'm at home in the dark," said Willie. "Just ask Mayo's ladies."

Several of the men laughed softly. Cole glanced at Hiram. The boy shoveled silently, a burlap sack at his feet. Cole felt Willie's eyes on him, but he ignored the surfman's stare.

Cole had left Antone Lucas to man the station. Before they left for the cemetery, Willie had come upstairs to Cole's quarters to ask that Hiram stay behind too. Willie had argued that even a blind man could see the girl's death had shaken the boy deeply; to have him dig her grave would be callous and uncaring, a sign that man was no better than the beasts. Cole had ignored the inference and the request. Death was part of their job. The sooner the boy grew accustomed to it, the better off he'd be. Hiram had walked the two miles to Provincetown cemetery with the rest of them.

Willie resumed digging, his mind on the boy. At seventeen, Hiram had already seen his share of life's fickle cruelty, but the boy still brimmed with energy and wonder. He was sad at times, and this was to be expected, but when he was absorbed in the present, he fairly boiled with curiosity and life. He reminded Willie of the electric ball that had careened through one of the station's windows during a lightning storm. The apparition had hummed about the station for an instant before buzzsawing back out the window, leaving everyone's hair on end. When Hiram joined the station as winter man two months earlier, hired to bolster manpower in a season that saw an average of two shipwrecks a week along the Cape's shore, he had infused the station with life. The men had taken to him instantly.

Since the wreck of the *Asia*, everyone had tried to shake Hiram from his gloom. Martin had baked a cherry pie, but the pie lay untouched for three days until Martin finally allowed the men to eat it. They tried cards with equivalent luck. Hiram was the luckiest card player any of them had seen, with consistent good fortune that would have been irritating and suspect in any other man. But Hiram didn't care whether he won or lost, and so his luck was endearing, though not to Antone, whose own luck with cards was equivalently bad. During calm weather, the two played poker deep into the night, matchsticks piling beside Hiram, hissed curses piling on Antone's lips.

Life, however, possessed an unfathomable deck: the boy had been dealt an unexpected card.

Maintaining a semblance of digging, Willie eyed the bodies curiously. Frost had turned every man pale, but they were still clearly sailors, their faces burnished by sun and wind, their hands scarred. The sole exception lay a short spit off Willie's right boot. The man was shaven-headed, with astonishingly large ears. Even in a frosted state, it was clear the elements had only recently gnawed his face raw. With the exception of a purpled coin-size mark in the center of his right palm, his hands were smooth, the nails tended. Fastidious to the end, the man had washed ashore wearing hand-sewn leather shoes and a silk vest, firmly buttoned. He was a good ten years older than any of his companions. Willie guessed the man was either an unlucky passenger or, more likely, a shipping company minion; perhaps an accountant, maybe even one of the ship's owners. Whoever he was, Willie doubted he had envisioned an end like this.

Willie felt sorry for the men, but he was more intrigued by the puzzle their bodies presented. By their youth and dress, all but the elephant-eared man were clearly sailors. But if the bald man had not been the captain, then one face was missing.

Under most circumstances it was not at all unusual for bodies to be lost to the sea. Given time, pushed by wind and current, bloated bodies often sailed off for the horizon. But the storm that had claimed the *Asia* had possessed an extraordinarily fierce northeast wind. The onshore wind, abetted by the tremendous surf, had driven virtually everything but the *Asia* herself ashore; the beach had been littered with lumber, tangles of rigging and sail, even a bilge pump that weighed the rough equivalent of an ox. Eventually, they would receive the crew list from the shipping company, but at the moment, it appeared one body had possibly bucked the elements, swaying now somewhere on the sea bottom.

Wherever he swayed, the missing man had at least escaped with his dignity. The *Asia's* crew was now outfitted for the circus. Once again, the Women's National Relief Association had provided burial vestments, and again no apparent accounting had been given to size. The largest sailors strained to burst their buttoned jackets, while the hands and feet of the smallest disappeared inside pants cuffs and jacket sleeves, as if they were already receding in death. It was true the Women's National Relief Association had limited means and could not provide for every variation of the human form. But it was also true the organization was comprised primarily of widows, many of whom had suffered unhappy marriages.

Done with the men, Willie's eyes walked the cemetery. Even by graveyard standards, Provincetown's final resting place was a sad and meager place; a half-acre of sandy dirt and wiry grass, treeless but for the solitary white oak at the cemetery's eastern edge. Headstones and wood crosses, canted at innumerable angles and stained like rotted teeth, drifted on the loamy rise and fall of land. There were no mausoleums or grand monuments. Times were never easy on the Cape. What money there was went to the living.

In Willie's mind, the cemetery possessed one saving grace: from its heights, it offered a resplendent view of Provincetown's steepled churches and jumbled buildings, and the wharves, lined with ships and skipjacks, poked like thumbs into Cape Cod Bay. Willie did not miss the humor in the cemetery's location. It perched, patient as any predator, gazing down on the bustle of ignorant victims.

Though few gave thought to their own inevitable residence, many enjoyed the prospect of seeing others lain to rest. For the past hour, a steady stream of townspeople had arrived in wagons and on foot. Nearly sixty people now stood murmuring in groups. Many came to pray because it was the duty of churchgoing folk, but it was also true that a dead child was rare.

Willie noted one conspicuous absence. Reverend Marmaduke Matthews was head of the Presbyterian Church. The largest church in Provincetown, its towering steeple pointed bright white into the sky, an illuminating finger reminding all that God watched their every move. Marmaduke Matthews was also Provincetown's largest minister. Within the walls of his church, the reverend, aided by his great bulk, issued booming scoldings, well-attended by the God-fearing. If one believed Marmaduke Matthews, hell was a crowded place, but the Devil had space enough remaining.

Reverend Matthews rarely bypassed a funeral or a crowd, both providing opportunity for driving yet another fiery lance of retribution into the rotting hearts of sinners. Still, Willie was fairly certain the good reverend would miss this chance. For reasons Willie had never fathomed, Captain Cole despised the minister, and the keeper's distaste, when openly manifested, provided a snort of brimstone itself. A funeral of today's magnitude would be a sore temptation, but Willie doubted the reverend had the nerve for it.

Daniel Cole noted Reverend Matthews' absence with relief. He detested religion as man had molded it. The ministers he had known lavished their attentions on the rich and the dead, distracting themselves, now and again, to berate the rest of the hard-working populace. They also prattled on, a particular inconvenience on a day as cold as this.

Cole saw he was not to escape aggravation entirely, however. As they finished squaring the mass grave, a tall figure cloaked in a black robe moved briskly in their direction. On the Cape, two things were certain: men died in shipwrecks, and Widow Addison Doane, doyenne of the Relief Association, oversaw their interment.

Widow Doane stepped up to Cole. She clasped a worn Bible in her hands. Although her frame was as spare as bamboo, her neck retained a repository of loose skin that, at this moment, swung from side to side as she took in the men.

"Keeper Cole, you'll bury the girl first."

Cole stood stiffly. "I will see to it."

Widow Doane nodded curtly. "You are a man who sees things through."

Cole held Widow Doane's gaze, but Willie saw his friend's knuckles whiten on the shovel. It wasn't just Widow Doane. Women made Daniel Cole uncomfortable. His friend had loved once, but now it was as if he had forgotten what to do in even the simplest circumstances.

Willie knew women found the keeper attractive. Though a head shorter than most men, he was square-shouldered and powerfully built, yet he retained the lithe movements and clear-sighted gaze of a boy scooping frogs from a creek. He considered the world through dark eyes made darker still by a shock of coal-black hair. The collective effect was one of sobriety and sadness. Women found sadness irresistible, and though they might swoon briefly at the feet of a romancer, in the end, seriousness was what their practical nature desired. Several of the whores Willie knew at the Cork and Barrel had expressed curiosity regarding the captain, and certain of the Cape's distinguished widows allowed word to circulate that they considered the keeper a worthy match. But Cole showed no interest in anyone. And that mute indifference had been instilled in a man whom women desired was, in Willie's mind, proof again that God liked things lively.

Widow Doane was not among Daniel Cole's admirers.

"Reverend Matthews will not be attending," she said. "I am assuming you will be conducting the service, Captain Cole?"

"Yes."

"I have prepared a sermon."

"It won't be necessary."

The widow dipped her chin slightly as if she might charge. Instead she said, "The girl is dressed in the dress we provided?"

"I saw to it myself."

"She looks natural?"

"As best as can be expected."

"Has she been marked in any fashion?"

"Only her legs."

The ache of not knowing shone in the widow's eyes. She waited, but Cole did not oblige.

"Her legs?" she said finally.

"They were broken."

"Poor child. Did she suffer greatly?"

"Only she could have told us."

"Are her injuries adequately concealed?"

"She is amply covered by the dress you supplied."

Willie peeked into the coffin. The dress was big enough for a grown woman. It bunched in great folds at the girl's feet, like a rose pedestal.

"The coffin is sufficient?" asked Widow Doane.

"Yes."

Widow Doane shot a tart glance in the direction of the undertaker, standing long-faced beside the beach cart.

"I hope that miserly man's needs are as simple when it comes time for his own funeral," she said, and with a cluck, Widow Doane departed.

Cole turned to the men.

"Place the shovels out of the way. We'll start the service in five minutes."

Hiram had absorbed the unfoldings with numb disinterest, but now the moment had come. Bending, he picked up the sack at his feet. Walking to the beach cart, he felt the brush of mourners, but for all he knew he was parting wheat. He ignored the skinny undertaker too. His hands and legs shook.

Hiram took the doll from the sack, the satin dress smooth against his fingers. He had washed the dress in a kitchen pot late one night, taking down the rusted iron and pressing it smooth. He placed the doll on the cart. The dishwater afternoon turned the bright red dress cheerier still. He stared at the doll for moment, the bald spot where the hair had been torn away, the lopsided smile, as if the left side of the mouth had assumed death's sadness.

Leaning over the coffin, Hiram willed his eyes wide. For a week now, the girl had tormented his dreams, her eyes probing his. Now her face was peaceful, and, with her eyes shut, accepting. Hiram knew this was another lie.

When he reached for the doll, it was gone.

"She's pretty," said a small voice. "Even bald."

Hiram could not breathe. His heart galloped in his chest.

He turned. He was not hearing the dead. The girl was no more than five. She stared up at him, nearly swallowed up in a pile of jackets and a woolen cap.

The doll swung in a mittened hand.

"Mother is afraid of the cold," she said. "My brother died of pneumonia. He was three. I'm wearing two pairs of wool knickers. They chafe."

Hiram tried to smile.

"You're Mrs. Parson's daughter," he said.

"I'm Emilia."

"Hello, Emilia."

The girl turned to the coffin.

"Are you her father?"

"No."

The round face lost and regained hope in almost the same instant.

"Is her father … *dead?*"

"Yes."

"What about her mother?"

"Her mother isn't here."

"Mother says women don't have to prove themselves by taking foolish chances at sea." The girl held the doll with both hands, studying it. She looked up at Hiram. "It's her doll?"

"Yes."

"But you have it now." The girl touched a chipped cheek gently. "You could give her to me."

He had vowed to do this one thing. To falter again would be almost laughable.

"The doll is all she has left. She needs it to help her rest."

"To help her *soul* rest. That … " the girl jerked a mittened thumb at the coffin, " … is food for worms." Her chapped lips pursed thoughtfully. "Her soul would know." The mittened hand rose. "I understand."

"Thank you," Hiram said, taking the doll.

"You're welcome." The girl tugged a corner of her wool cap. "She can't speak anymore," she said, and disappeared into the crowd.

Hiram nearly called after her. He was a coward and a fool. The dead had no use for dolls. If the girl could speak, she would laugh at him. Leaning over the casket, he placed the doll gently in the crook of an arm. The doll smiled up at him, but the girl did not.

They buried the girl first. Pale sunlight bathed the cemetery in apathetic light, but in the shadows thrown by the oak's thickest branches, evening already held sway. The living shivered. The floor of the grave was already glazed with frost.

Cole had fashioned a cross, whittling two pieces of birch to clean white bone and fixing them together with fishing line. Bending, he drove the cross into the jumbled earth.

Willie and Martin placed the coffin beside the grave. The mourners pressed forward, jockeying for a glimpse.

Cole had wanted the coffin shut, but Widow Doane had insisted the coffin remain open until it was lowered into the grave; the gathered, she said, should know the heartless capriciousness of the devil sea. Cole thought the sentiment ridiculous, like showcasing a plough for farmers, but he kept silent. Having once denied Widow Doane the chance to speak, he had realized the danger of forcing her to relent again.

Willie and the Swede slid the lid into place. Willie nailed the lid shut. The hammering in the frozen stillness was sharp and loud. Several mourners, veterans of the war, hunched at the first report. Then the surfmen lowered the casket with ropes, bumping it to rest.

After the sailors had been rolled as delicately as possible into their mass grave, Cole spoke.

"These sailors knew the risks of their profession. Their deaths were a risk willingly shouldered. The sadness here is in the loved ones left behind."

Cole bowed his head.

The mourners, caught off guard by the brevity of the sermon, shuffled and whispered before following suit. A child giggled.

Widow Doane began reciting the Lord's Prayer.

Cole spoke over her.

"Children are a different matter. They do not choose their fate." Cole watched for a moment as the oak's thinner branches, nudged by the freshening wind, assumed a mocking bob. "Someone had their reasons for taking this child to sea in winter. May they live with those reasons in whatever eternity awaits them."

Cole turned to the surfmen.

"Fill in the graves."

*Thank you very much for reading. If you're curious about the rest of the tale, Fog is available in soft cover, hard back and e-book at Amazon, iUniverse or wherever e-books are sold.*

*I appreciate each and every reader.*

*Gratefully, Ken McAlpine*

www.kenmcalpine.com
www.facebook.com/kenmcalpineauthor

## ABOUT THE AUTHOR

Ken McAlpine is the author of ten books; fiction, non-fiction and selected essays. His books and magazine articles have received numerous awards. Of his novel TOGETHER WE JUMP, USA Today said, "There's a beautiful Forrest Gump feel to this book. The main character was a delight and I just loved his sad, wistful, wonderful tale." His non-fiction work OFF SEASON: DISCOVERING AMERICA ON WINTER'S SHORE was a Barnes and Noble Discover Great New Writers selection.

Ken's magazine articles have earned three Lowell Thomas awards, travel writing's top award. More important to him, assignments from magazines ranging from National Geographic Traveler to Sunset, have provided him unbridled opportunity for play: from diving with white sharks, to running the Inca trail to Machu Picchu, to sparring with the world shoot fighting champion (you cannot learn a martial art in a week).

Most important, Ken lives in Ventura, California with his wife and their two sons. He likes to stand in his yard at night looking at the stars, but he does not like to spend any time during the day doing yard work.

www.ingramcontent.com/pod-product-compliance
Lightning Source LLC
Chambersburg PA
CBHW070644130626
46555CB00006B/2703